MYRO and the Skydivers

Belongs to ....

Also available...

Audio CD
Myro, The Smallest Plane In The World

Songs and Music CD

MYRO
The Smallest Plane In The World

Listen to the song!

Myro and the Skydivers
Book 5 from Series 1: Myro Goes to Australia

First published October 2010 by NickRose Ltd
www.nickrose.com
ISBN 978-1-907972-04-1

Myro's Team
Concept and Story: Nick Rose
Illustrations and Branding: Lucy Corrina Bourn
Designer: Sue Mason
Writer: Fiona Veitch Smith
Editor: Mary O'Riordan
Editorial Consultant: Samantha Mackintosh
Australian Consultant: Jane Massam
3D Consultancy: Jon Stuart and Sean Frisby
Project Management: Nick Rose
Continue the fun at www.myro.com

nr.
nickrose ltd

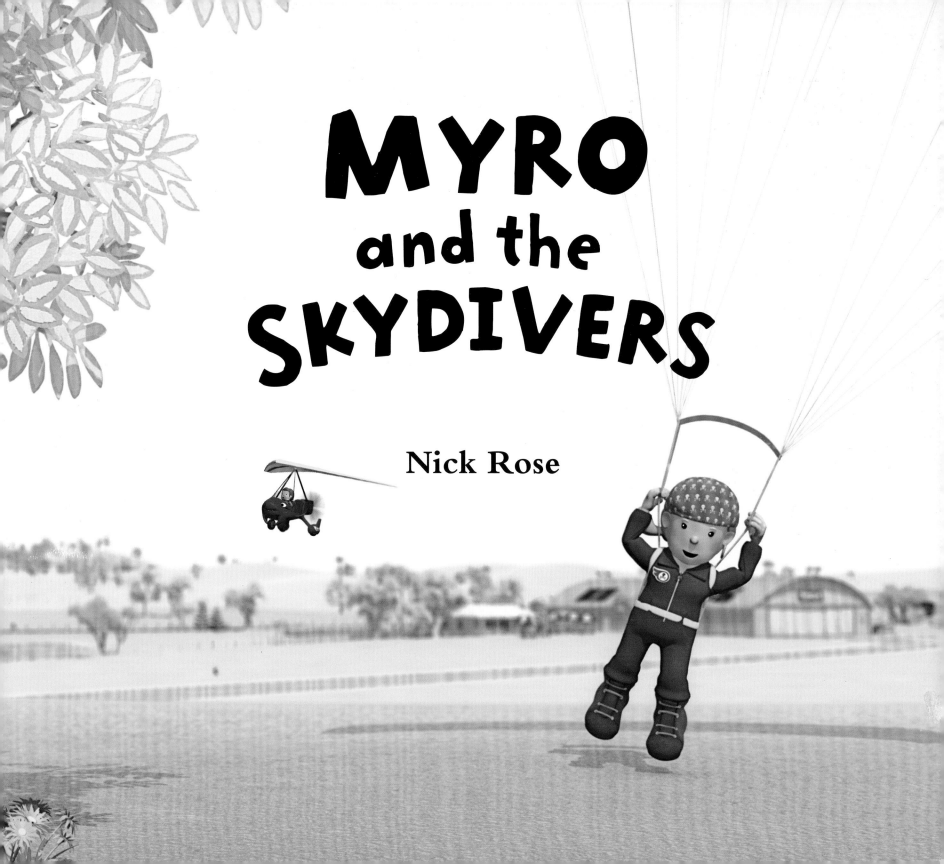

MYRO
and the
SKYDIVERS

Nick Rose

Myro the microlight is
the smallest plane in the world . . .

. . . and he loves to fly in the
Australian Bush.

Everything is new and exciting
and so different from his home in the UK.

Early one morning when there wasn't a breath
of wind in the sky, Myro saw a small airfield
with a big cross painted near the runway.
In the middle of the cross,
a red flare was smoking brightly.

"I wonder if someone's in trouble?" said Myro.
"We'd better check it out," replied
Michael, his pilot.

Myro lined up with the runway and made
his approach. But as he came in to land he saw
a skull and crossbones painted on the roof of the hangar!

"Pirates!" exclaimed Myro.
"Let's get out of here!"

"There's no such thing as pirates, Myro,"
laughed Michael.

Although Myro's wing was wobbling with worry, he managed to land safely.

"That's odd," said Michael, "there's no one here."

"But who lit the flare?" asked Myro. "Maybe they're hiding from the pirates, desperate to be rescued!"

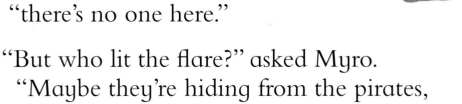

Suddenly Myro heard the faraway roar of a
Dakota's engines. He looked up and . . .

. . . oh no!

Pirates!

Loads of them!
Jumping out of the enormous
aeroplane and diving through
the sky!

They grabbed hold of each
other's hands and feet
to make a skull and
crossbones in the sky.

Myro couldn't believe his eyes.

All at once they broke apart and out popped their parachutes. They began drifting down to Myro and Michael . . .

closer . . .

and closer . . .

and closer!

"They're heading straight for us," squeaked Myro, "and it's too late to hide!"

The pirates landed around the coloured flare, pulled in
their parachutes and started folding them up.
And that's when the biggest pirate of the lot spotted them.

"Hey! Little microlight!
What are you doing here?"
he yelled.

"Uh-oh!" said Michael.
"Now we're in trouble!"

"I told you this was a pirate hideout!" yelped Myro.

"We're not real pirates, we're skydivers!" chuckled a lady called Penny.

"Then why do you have a skull and crossbones on your clothes and on your hangar?" asked Myro.

"Because we call ourselves the Parachute Pirates," she explained.

"Do you look for treasure?"
asked Myro.

"Of course! It's at the end
of the rainbow!"
shouted the pirates cheerfully.

Myro laughed and they all began to
chat before a huge noise drowned
out their voices.

Myro screwed up his eyes as Deko the Dakota came in to land.

This aeroplane had been made in the USA. He was **BIG** and **LOUD** and raised more dust than a herd of cattle stampeding for a billabong.

"Why's there a flying lawnmower on my runway?"
Deko boomed with a cheeky smile on his face.

"This is Myro the microlight," said Penny, "the smallest plane in the world!"

"Ha! Real planes are big, like me. I bet he's too small to drop a skydiver from the clouds," replied Deko with a swagger.

"He's not too small!" defended Penny.

"In fact," Penny continued,
"another jump would be ripper! Will you take me up, Myro?"

Myro looked at Michael hopefully.
"Can we?" he asked.

"Nope," answered Michael, "we need
permission from our manager and I don't
know where she is."

Myro's wingtips drooped.
"Pleeeeease!" Penny begged.

Michael laughed,
"Well . . . OK,
just one jump."

Although Myro knew he was being naughty,
he wanted to show that Dakota what he was made of.

He took off at full speed and pushed his wing as far forward as he could.

"Higher!" Penny cried. "You need to go higher!"

So Myro climbed
up, up, and up
into the air!

He flew closer to the sun than
he'd ever flown before!

When the pirates' hangar
was just a dot beneath them,
Myro turned his engine off.

All they could hear was the
whoosh of air over his wing as
they glided across the sky.

"Whoopee!" cried Penny
as she jumped out, hurtling
towards the earth . . .

stretching . . .

spinning . . .

diving . . .

. . . until at last she threw out her
arms and legs to slow her fall.

Penny flew through a cloud,
released her parachute and floated
gently to the ground.

Then just as Myro turned his engine back on
a loud voice came over the radio.

"Myro the microlight, **land immediately!**"

Oh no!

Myro was in big trouble now.

He'd been so busy watching
Penny skydiving that he hadn't seen
Cylo the Cessna flying nearby.
And Cylo was carrying Madge,
the Flying Club manager!

Myro landed in two shakes of a lamb's tail, closely followed by an angry Cylo. Madge stormed over. She was REALLY cross!

She told them exactly why
they were in such trouble.

"*Sorry,*" whispered Myro,
but the day was spoiled.

Myro's wing was taken off
and he was sent straight
to his hangar.

The clouds turned dark
and it rained and
rained all night long.

The next morning
Michael came
to see Myro.

MYRO

"I'm sorry about all the trouble yesterday," he said.

"It was my fault too," said Myro, cheering up.
"I knew I should have said no, but –"

CARAAANG!

The little microlight jumped in surprise as the hangar doors were shoved open . . .

And in walked Penny the pirate! "I'm sorry too, boys, I shouldn't have nagged you into taking me."

Madge the manager was just behind her.

"Because you all know that what you did yesterday was wrong, I thought you may like to go skydiving again, but this time with my permission."

Myro couldn't believe his luck!

With the rain clearing,
they zoomed off,
Myro climbing as high
as he could.

Suddenly he noticed a rainbow.

"There could be treasure,"
he called to Penny.

"Too right!" she shouted,
leaping out of the microlight.

Myro laughed as he
swooped a swoop and followed
the parachutist down to earth . . .

stretching . . .

spinning . . .

diving . . .

with rainbow colours flashing like
pirate treasure over his wing the whole way down.

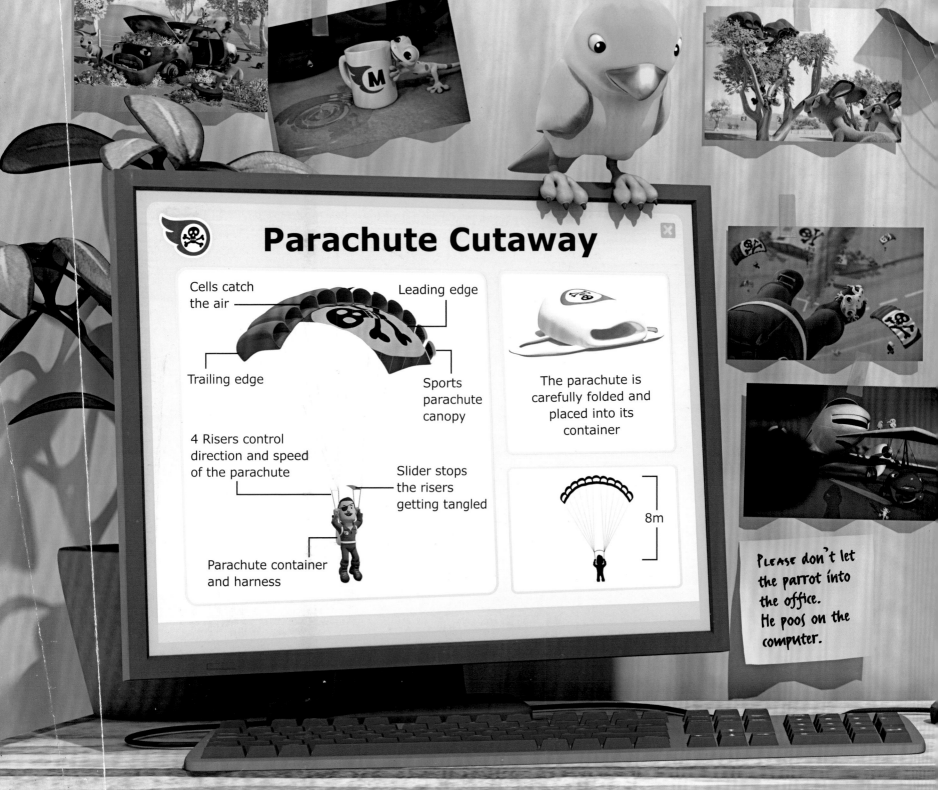